Don't Be Scared, Little Lamb!

Written by Moira Butterfield.
Illustrated by Rachael O'Neill.

DERRYDALE BOOKS
New York

Evening has come and the Little Farm is quiet. The farmer has gone home to have his dinner and the animals will soon be going to sleep.

Little Lamb is in the farmyard. He is shaking inside his woolly coat! "I don't like it getting dark," he says. "I'm scared of all the shadows!"

When Little Lamb peeks through the barn door he sees a scary shadow moving around inside. "Help, there's a monster!" he cries.

Then Little Puppy pokes his head around the door. "That's not a monster's shadow; that's mine!" he says. "I was just exploring inside the barn."

When Little Lamb looks in the farmyard he sees another scary shadow creeping around. "Help, there's a ghost!" he cries.

Then Little Hen jumps up from a bale of hay. "That's not a ghost's shadow; that's mine!" she says. "I was just looking for a place to sleep."

When Little Lamb looks into his pen
he sees another scary shadow coming
towards him. "Help, there's a giant!"
he cries.

Little Lamb runs round and round his pen. Then . . . CRASH! He bumps right into the farmer! "Help, there's a giant chasing after me!" cries Little Lamb.

"That's not a giant's shadow; that's mine!"
says the farmer. "I was just taking a walk
before bedtime. You're being very silly,
Little Lamb!"

"I'm so scared of shadows," says Little Lamb. "What shall I do?" "Come with me," replies the farmer. "I'll show you why you shouldn't be afraid."

The farmer takes Little Lamb into a shadowy corner. "There's nothing to be scared of here," he says. "Ask the spider. This is where she lives."

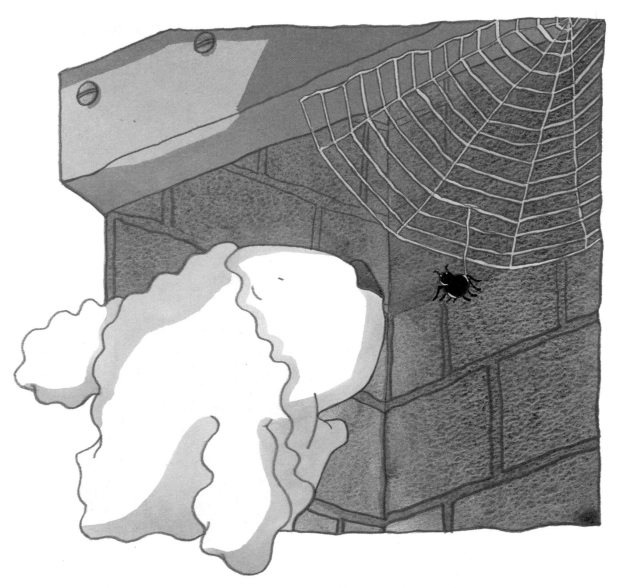

A little tiny spider is hanging from a thread. "Do you like this shadow?" asks Little Lamb. "Yes, it makes a nice cozy home," replies the spider.

The farmer takes Little Lamb into another dark corner. "There's nothing to be scared of here," he says. "Ask the owl. This is where he lives."

A fluffy, wide-eyed owl is perching on a
box. "Do you like this shadow?" asks Little
Lamb. "Yes, it makes a nice quiet home,"
says the owl.

The farmer takes Little Lamb into another dark corner. "There's nothing to be scared of here," he says. "Ask the mouse. This is where she lives."

A little grey mouse is curled up on some straw. "Do you like this shadow?" asks Little Lamb. "Yes, it makes a nice safe home," replies the mouse.

"You see, you don't need to be scared, Little Lamb," says the farmer. "There are no monsters or ghosts or giants to chase you on this farm!"

"Thank you, I feel much better," says Little Lamb. "But there is still something chasing me, you know." "Whatever is it now?" sighs the farmer.

"It follows me wherever I go, but I'd be VERY silly if I was scared of it," laughs Little Lamb. "Look — it's my very own shadow!"